This book belongs to:

To Remi MM
For Jinny, for everything AD

First published in Great Britain in 2005 by Andersen Press Ltd., 20 Vauxhall Bridge Road, London SW1V 2SA.
This paperback edition first published in 2006 by Andersen Press Ltd.
Published in Australia by Random House Australia Pty., Level 3, 100 Pacific Highway, North Sydney, NSW 2060.
Text copyright © 2005 by Alan Durant. Illustrations copyright © 2005 by Mei Matsuoka.
Text and cover design by David Mackintosh.

Printed and bound in Italy by Grafiche AZ, Verona.

10   9   8   7   6   5   4   3   2

British Library Cataloguing in Publication Data available.

ISBN 978 1 84270 537 7

This book has been printed on acid-free paper.

BURGER BOY

Alan Durant   Mei Matsuoka

Andersen Press
London

Benny didn't like vegetables.

He didn't like carrots.
He didn't like peas.

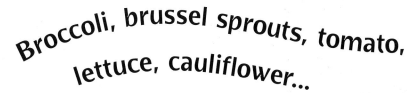

Broccoli, brussel sprouts, tomato, lettuce, cauliflower...

Benny didn't care for any of these.

Benny liked burgers. Benny LOVED burgers.
Burgers were the only food that Benny would eat.

**"You'll turn into a
burger one day,"**
his mum
warned.

And one day, Benny did.

When he came out of Bigger Burgers
a dog ran up and started to sniff.
Mmm, he loved the smell of Benny: what a tasty whiff!
He opened his mouth and yum yum yum...

"Look out, RUN, Benny!" cried his mum.

Benny jumped just in time and raced away down the street with the dog close behind greedy for his meat.

"I'm not a burger, I'm a boy!" shouted Benny. "Let me be!"

But that dog kept on chasing and, soon,
one became two, three,
then four,
five, six, seven,
eight, nine, ten...

All howling and hollering as they hounded poor Ben.

Benny ran into a field that was full of cows.
I'll shelter here, he thought. I'll be safe now.

But the cows mooed angrily. Said Benny, "What's the fuss?"
The cows swished their tails and said,
"Don't you know what burgers are made of? US!"

Benny was off again,
running through fields and over a stream
with a pack of dogs and a herd of cows chasing after him.

Benny saw a group of boys playing ball.
"Help," he gasped. "Save me, I'm in trouble!"

The boys stopped playing.
They looked, they stared,
they couldn't believe their eyes.

Poor Benny!

Off he ran again up and down a hill.

chased by dogs and cows and now hungry boys as well.

When...

Oh no! A busy road blocked his way.
Benny was trapped.
He couldn't go forward, he couldn't go back.
He was about to become
a giant burger snack!

But then... a van screeched suddenly to a stop.
"Want a lift?" called the driver. "Quick! In you hop!"

At last, I'm safe, thought Benny, as he rode in that big white van.
But little did he know it'd take him right back to
where his nightmare began!

The man carried Benny into Bigger Burgers
And with a voice as cold as ice, said,

**"Roll up for a taste of
my super burger,
only a pound a slice."**

"I'm not
a burger,
I'm a boy!"
shouted Benny.
"Let me be!"

"A talking burger!"
laughed the man.
"Why, I'll charge
twice the price."

Things looked bad for Benny.
The knife was about to cut into his bun,
When... his mum ran in and shouted,

"Don't touch that burger, he's my son!"

She took Benny home

and fed him with fruit
and with veg,

and slowly his burger body
turned boyish at the edge.

"I'm a boy again!"
cried Benny.
"I'm cured,
hooray, hooray!"

"**I'll never ever eat
another burger
from this day."**

And Benny didn't.

Carrots, cauliflower, lettuce, broccoli, peas...

Vegetables like these were all that he would eat.

He loved the stuff! He couldn't get enough.

Now he gorged on vegetables, as once he'd gorged on meat.

His mum was worried.

"Benny," she warned. "You'd better be careful, son.
If you only eat vegetables like that, then one day..."

you'll turn into one!"

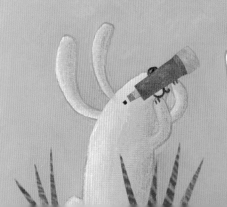

Praise for

BuRGER BOy

"Witty rhymes and sprightly illustrations, will definitely entertain everyone." **EVENING STANDARD**

"The dangers of eating too much junk food (too much of anything, as it turns out) have rarely been so entertainingly and memorably stated." **SCOTSMAN**

"Great fun!"
MOTHER AND BABY

"The illustrations are fantastic, and Benny's transformation into a burger and bun is hilarious . . . There's also a neat twist at the end making this a great culinary cautionary tale."
myBooksmag